FLINT PUBLIC LIBRA
W9-BXR-234

Old Pig

For my Mother
M.W.

Special Thanks to Rosalind Price,
to Margaret, Sam, Adelaide and Henry,
and to Paul Clark for Captain Taylor's paddock
R.B.

Old Pig
Story by Margaret Wild
Pictures by Ron Brooks
Dial Books for Young Readers
NEW YORK

Old Pig and Granddaughter had lived together for a long, long time.

They shared everything,
including the chores.

Every day Granddaughter chopped the wood,
while Old Pig cleaned out the fire grate.

Granddaughter swept, while Old Pig dusted.

Old Pig made the beds, while Granddaughter hung up the wash.

Granddaughter made porridge, toast, and tea for breakfast.

Old Pig diced carrots and turnips for lunch.

And together Old Pig and Granddaughter prepared their dinner of corn and oats.

"I hate corn and oats," Granddaughter always said.

And Old Pig always replied, "Corn and oats are good for you. While I'm alive, my dear, you'll eat them up."

At that, Granddaughter stopped complaining. She'd eat corn and oats for breakfast, lunch, and dinner if it meant that Old Pig would live forever.

One morning Old Pig did not get up for breakfast as usual.

"I'm feeling tired," she said. "I think I'll have breakfast in bed today."

"But you never eat in bed!" said Granddaughter. "You don't like getting crumbs in the sheets."

"I'm tired," Old Pig repeated.

When Granddaughter brought her a tray of porridge, toast, and tea, Old Pig was already asleep, and she slept through lunch and dinner too.

While Old Pig slept, Granddaughter chopped the wood, cleaned out the fire grate, swept, dusted, did the wash, and made her bed. She tried to whistle while she worked but all she could manage was a lonely little "oink."

The next morning Old Pig was still tired, but she made herself get up. She had a spoonful of porridge, a bite of toast, and a sip of tea.

"That's not enough to feed a sparrow, let alone a grown-up pig like you," said Granddaughter. She made a stern face, but Old Pig just shut her eyes for a moment, then looked around for her bag and hat.

"I have a lot to do today," she said. "I must be prepared."
"Prepared for what?" asked Granddaughter.

Old Pig didn't reply. She didn't have to. Granddaughter already knew the answer, and it made her feel like crying inside.

Old Pig returned her books to the library—and didn't borrow any more. She went to the bank, took out all her money, and closed the account.

Then she went to the grocery store and paid the bill. She also paid the electricity bill, the telephone bill, and the bill for firewood.

When she got home, she tucked the rest of her money into Granddaughter's purse. "Keep it safe," she said, "and use it wisely."

"I will," said Granddaughter. She tried to smile but her mouth wobbled, and Old Pig said, "There, there, no tears."

"I promise," said Granddaughter, but it was the hardest promise she'd ever made.

"Now," said Old Pig, "I want to feast."
"You've got your appetite back?" Granddaughter asked, suddenly feeling hopeful.
"I'm not hungry for food," Old Pig said. "I want to take a slow walk around the town and feast my eyes on the trees, the flowers, the sky—on everything!"

So Old Pig and Granddaughter went for a slow walk around the town. Every now and then Old Pig had to stop and rest. But she kept on looking. Looking and listening, smelling and tasting.

"Look!" said Old Pig.
"Do you see how the light glitters on the leaves?"

"Look!" said Old Pig.
"Do you see how the clouds gather like gossips in the sky?"

"Look!" said Old Pig.
"Do you see how the trees are reflected in the lake?"

"Do you hear the parrots quarreling?
Can you smell the warm earth?
Let's taste the rain!"

It was late by the time Old Pig and Granddaughter got home.

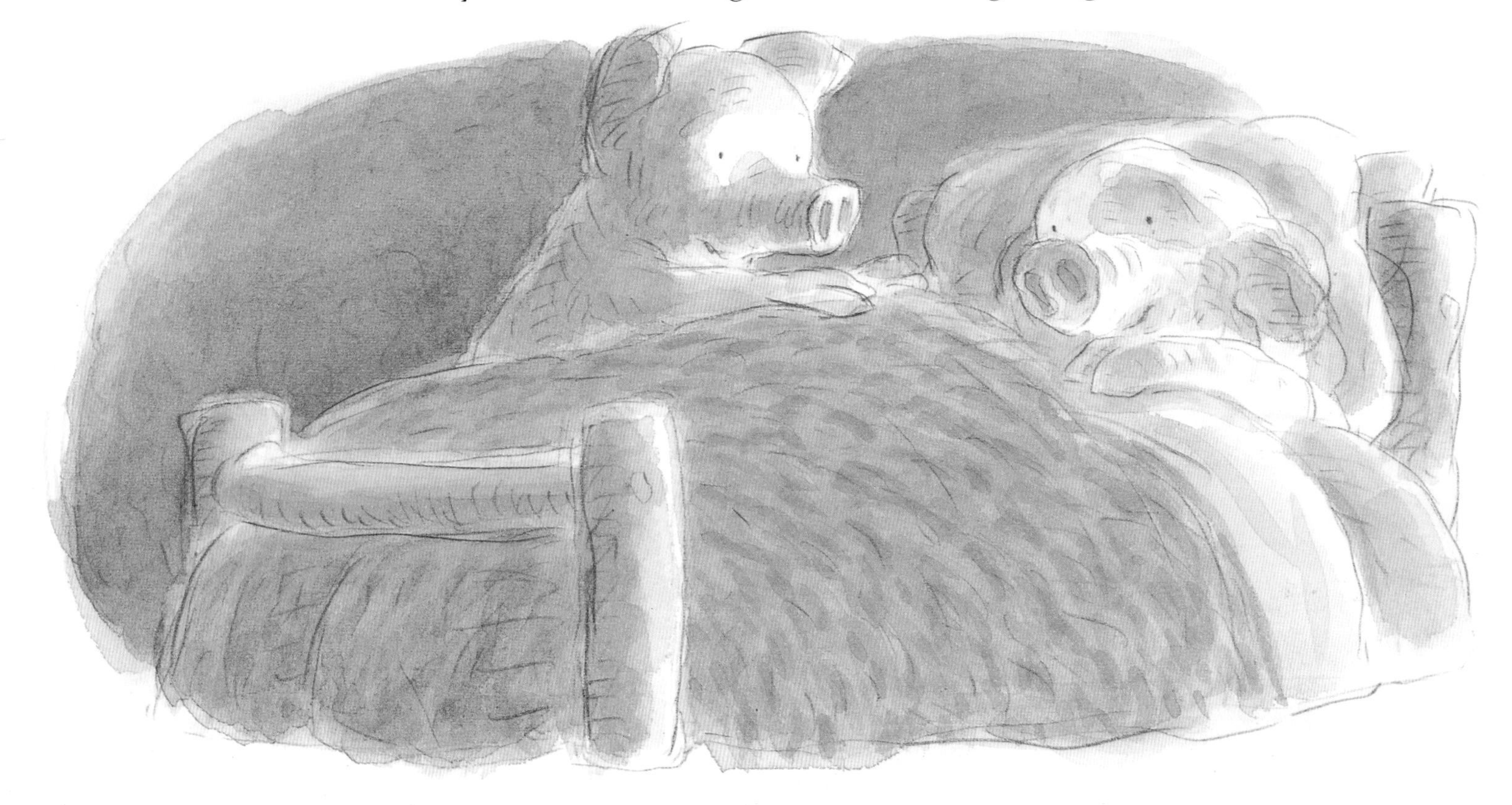

Old Pig was so exhausted that Granddaughter helped her right into bed.

Then Granddaughter made herself a bowl of corn and oats, and she ate them all up. She washed the dishes and put them away.

Then she went into Old Pig's room. Old Pig was not yet asleep.

Granddaughter sat beside her on the bed. She said, "Do you remember when I was little and had a bad dream, you used to come into my bed and hold me tight?"
"I remember," said Old Pig.

"Tonight," said Granddaughter, "I'd like to come into your bed and hold you tight. Would that be all right?".
"That would be very all right," said Old Pig.

So Granddaughter switched off the lights, and opened the window to let in the breeze and opened the curtains to let in the moon.

Then she climbed into Old Pig's bed. She put her arms around Old Pig, and for the very last time Old Pig and Granddaughter held each other tight until morning.

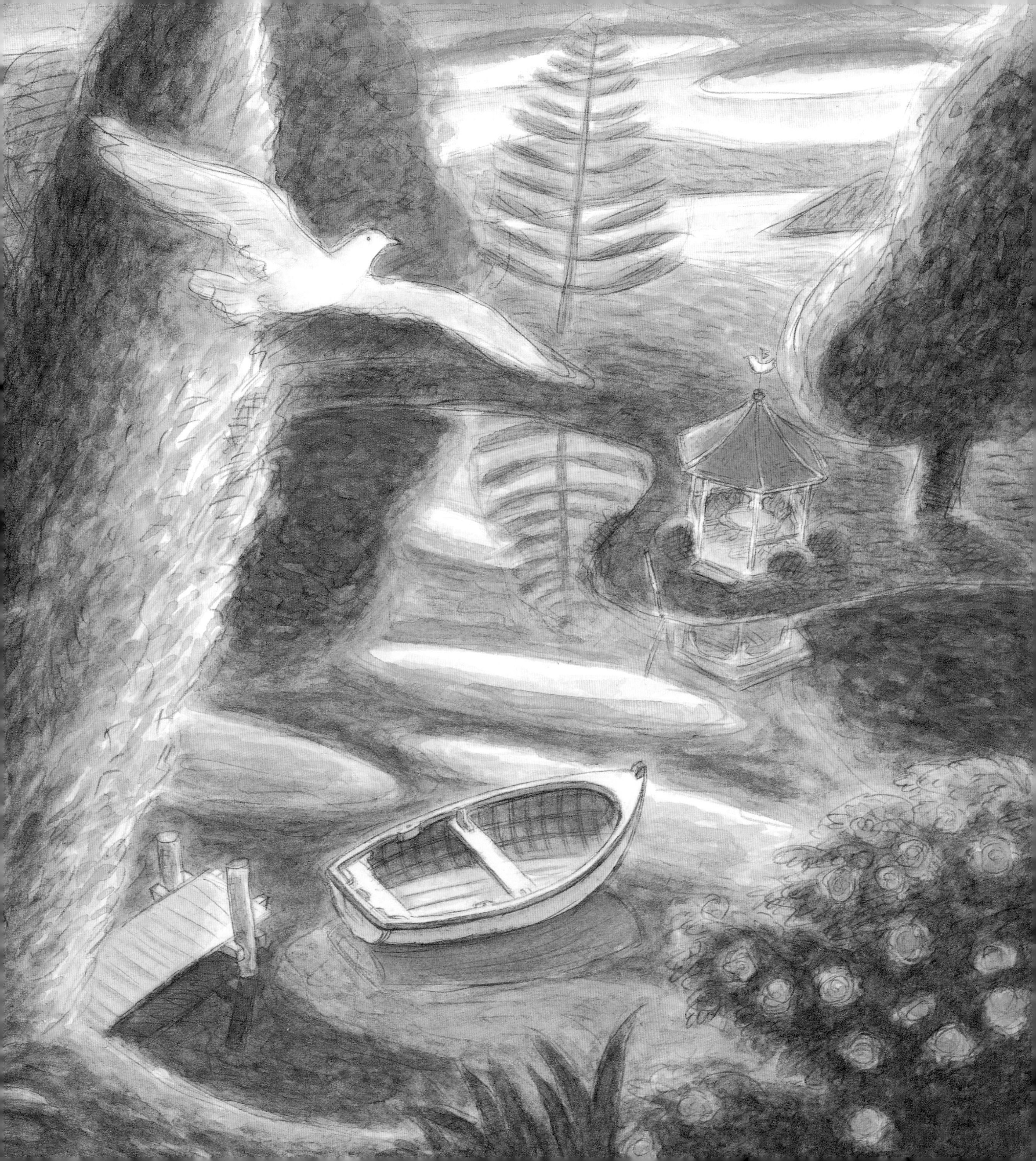

First published in the United States 1996 by
Dial Books for Young Readers
A Division of Penguin Books USA Inc.
375 Hudson Street
New York, New York 10014
Published in Australia 1995 by
Allen & Unwin Pty Ltd

Printed by Toppan Printing Company, Singapore
First Edition
1 3 5 7 9 10 8 6 4 2

Library of Congress Cataloging in Publication Data
Wild, Margaret, 1948–
Old Pig / story by Margaret Wild;
pictures by Ron Brooks.—1st ed.
p. cm.
"Published in Australia 1995 by
Allen & Unwin Pty Ltd"—T.p. verso.
Summary: Because Old Pig knows that her time
to die is near, she puts her affairs in order and takes
a slow walk with Granddaughter to savor
the beauty for one last time.
ISBN 0-8037-1917-5 (hardcover)
[1. Pigs—Fiction. 2. Death—Fiction.]
I. Brooks, Ron, ill. II. Title.
PZ7.W6457401 1996 [E]—dc20 95-668 CIP AC

The illustrations for this book were created
with pencil and watercolor.